Sweet Surprises

written by David J. Fiday

illustrated by Christina Rigo

Library of Congress Catalog Card No. 88-63570
© 1989, The STANDARD PUBLISHING Company, Cincinnati, Ohio
Division of STANDEX INTERNATIONAL Corporation. Printed in U.S.A.

As soon as Julie awoke, she made her
bed. Then she was smiling when Mom
peeked in the door.

"Did you make your bed all by
yourself?" Mom asked.

"Yes," said Julie. "I'm a big girl now!"

"That's a sweet surprise," Mom said,
smiling.

"What's a sweet surprise?" asked
Julie.

"A sweet surprise is a little help that
you weren't expecting to get," said
Mom. "Someone sweet thinks of it all
by herself!"

Julie thought about sweet surprises as she ate her breakfast. When she finished her cereal and toast, she put her dishes in the sink to surprise her mom.

That's two sweet surprises for Mom today, Julie thought.

She went outside to find more sweet
surprises that she could do. And as she
looked around, she saw all the toys she
hadn't put away the day before. A third
sweet surprise popped into her head.
She would put her toys away so Mom
wouldn't have to.

But, as Julie was putting her bicycle away, sand spilled all over her clean pants! She tried to brush it off.

Then Julie saw that her dad had forgotten to put away a rake and some grass bags. She thought of a fourth sweet surprise. She would put Dad's rake and the bags away for him.

But when she put them away, a shovel fell over and mud splattered on her arm.

But Julie soon forgot about the mud when she found her brother's lost tennis ball in a dark corner of the garage. She knew it would be sweet surprise number five if she put it back in his room.

But when she tried to put the ball into her pocket, Julie pushed too hard. Her pocket ripped. So she ran indoors to put it back.

When Julie came back outside, she noticed that Lulu, the dog next door, was tangled up in her leash.

Lulu needs a sweet surprise, thought Julie as she went through the gate to help her. Lulu was so happy to be free, she gave Julie a big wet doggie kiss. Then she jumped up and put two big muddy paw prints on Julie's blouse.

Julie only rubbed Lulu's head and smiled as she thought, *sweet surprise number six. Maybe I can find four more and make it ten.*

Julie noticed Lulu's empty water bowl.

"Lulu, you need one more sweet surprise and that makes seven," said Julie. So she used a garden hose to fill Lulu's bowl.

Some of the water splashed over
Julie's new tennis shoes, but she just
laughed and rubbed Lulu's head again.

When Julie turned off the water, she noticed three big weeds growing by the faucet. If she pulled the weeds, it would be sweet surprise number eight.

As she pulled on the weeds, green plant juice covered her hands. Julie rubbed them on her pants.

She said good-bye to Lulu as she went back to her own yard, looking for sweet surprise number nine.

Julie thought her mom's flowers in the front yard needed water. She turned on the hose and gave them a drink. Then she smiled. She had found sweet surprise number nine.

But as Julie watered Mom's flowers, mud splashed up against her shoes and pants.

Then Julie heard her mom calling. She began running and slipped on the wet sidewalk and fell down. Mom picked her up and found Julie had torn a hole in her pants.

"Julie, Julie, just look at you!" said Mom. "What have you been doing?"

"I've been looking for sweet surprises," said Julie with a grin. "I found nine. I only need one more to have ten."

"What kind of sweet surprises make a little girl so dirty? Don't you think you need a bath and clean clothes?" said Mom.

Julie laughed and hurried to her room. While she undressed, Mom filled the tub. Julie was surprised when she saw the tub filled with a mountain of bubbles.

"Aren't bubbles only for Saturday night baths?" asked Julie.

"Usually," said Mom, "but you made your bed this morning, and that was a sweet surprise for me. I thought you should have a sweet surprise too."

Then Mom put a big pile of bubbles on Julie's head.

That's sweet surprise number ten and it's for me! thought Julie.

"Now, Julie," Mom said, "will you tell
me all about your sweet surprises?"

"Do you promise not to tell anybody?"
asked Julie.

"Yes, I promise," said Mom.

Then Julie told her every one of her
ten sweet surprises.